WELCOME TO
PASSPORT TO READING
A beginning reader's ticket to a brand-new world!

Every book in this program is designed to build read-along and read-alone skills, level by level, through engaging and enriching stories. As the reader turns each page, he or she will become more confident with new vocabulary, sight words, and comprehension.

These PASSPORT TO READING levels will help you choose the perfect book for every reader.

READING TOGETHER
Read short words in simple sentence structures together to begin a reader's journey.

READING OUT LOUD
Encourage developing readers to sound out words in more complex stories with simple vocabulary.

READING INDEPENDENTLY
Newly independent readers gain confidence reading more complex sentences with higher word counts.

READY TO READ MORE
Readers prepare for chapter books with fewer illustrations and longer paragraphs.

This book features sight words from the educator-supported Dolch Sight Word List. Readers will become more familiar with these commonly used vocabulary words, increasing reading speed and fluency.

For more information, please visit www.passporttoreadingbooks.com, where each reader can add stamps to a personalized passport while traveling through story after story!

Enjoy the journey!

Little, Brown and Company

Hachette Book Group
237 Park Avenue, New York, NY 10017
Visit our website at www.lb-kids.com

Little, Brown and Company is a division of Hachette Book Group, Inc.
The Little, Brown name and logo are trademarks of Hachette Book Group, Inc.

The publisher is not responsible for websites (or their content) that are not owned by the publisher.

First Edition: September 2012

ISBN 978-0-316-18310-9

10 9 8 7 6 5 4 3 2

CW

Printed in the United States of America

Book design by Maria Mercado

Passport to Reading titles are leveled by independent reviewers applying the standards developed by Irene Fountas and Gay Su Pinnell in *Matching Books to Readers: Using Leveled Books in Guided Reading*, Heinemann, 1999.

THE MUPPETS

Presto, Gonzo!

by Lucy Rosen
illustrated by Kory Heinzen

LITTLE, BROWN AND COMPANY
New York   Boston

Hi, Muppet fans!

Can you find these things in this book?

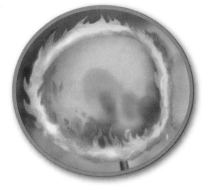

RING OF FIRE

MOTORCYCLE

TOP HAT

VAT OF PUDDING

It is time for dress rehearsal
at the Muppet Theater.
The Great Gonzo
is practicing his act.

"I, The Great Gonzo,
will perform the most
fantastic stunt ever,"
Gonzo announces from the stage.

"I will now jump over this cow
on my motorcycle, through a ring of fire,
while singing 'Old MacDonald Had a Farm'
and juggling some chickens."

"Lights, please," Gonzo says.

Nothing happens.

"I said, lights, please!" Gonzo yells.

But still the stage is dark.

Gonzo steps off the motorcycle,
and the chickens land.
"Excuse me, ladies," he says.
"I need to go find Scooter."

Gonzo finds Scooter by the light controls.
"Scooter, you missed your cue!" he exclaims.

"Oh, sorry, Gonzo,"
Scooter apologizes.
"I am reading this book
about Harry Houdini.
I must have lost track of your act."

"Harry who?" asks Gonzo.

"You know," says Scooter,

"the great magician!

He could get free from any trap."

"Houdini once escaped from a giant milk can filled with water with his hands tied behind his back," Scooter tells him.

"Cool! Sounds like my kind of guy," replies Gonzo.

"Call off the rest of my rehearsal,"
Gonzo says to Scooter.
"At tomorrow's show,
I will spice up my act
with some magic!"

"I hope those chickens like hot sauce," says Statler.

"Why?" asks Waldorf.

"Because they will need more than magic to spice up that act! Ha ha!"

The next day, Gonzo wears a top hat and a cape.

"I am Gonzo the Great Magician!

Watch as I pull a hare out of a hat while

dancing across the Tightrope of Doom!"

Camilla, wearing rabbit ears,
pops out of the top hat!
"Hare today," Gonzo says, doing a jig.
He pushes Camilla back down into the hat.
"Gone tomorrow!" he cries. "Ta-da!"
Gonzo loses his balance. *Crash!*
"I meant to do that," he wails.

"Bawk bawk ba-gawk!" Camilla squawks.

"Bless you," says Gonzo. "Have a hankie."

Camilla pulls Gonzo's handkerchief.

A dozen colorful scarves come out!

Camilla pulls and pulls.

The last scarf has a snake tied to it.

"Gonzo the Great Magician will hypnotize this poisonous python," says Gonzo.
"Look into my eyes," he says to the python.
"I do not think sssssso," hisses the snake.
"Aah!" Gonzo cries, and runs away.

"For my next trick," says Gonzo, peeking out from behind the curtain, "I will step into the Box of Doom and disappear into thin air."

"Is that a promise?" Statler asks.

Statler and Waldorf laugh.

Gonzo gets inside the box.

Camilla spins it around three times.

POOF!

A thick cloud of smoke appears.

Camilla opens the door.

Gonzo is still there,

with black smudges on his face.

"A little too much powder,"

he says with a cough.

"And now, the grand finale," says Gonzo.
"I call it Gonzo's Great Escape!
I, The Great Gonzo, will be handcuffed
high in the air, above a vat of pudding.
I must get free before I am lowered
into the Tapioca Tub of Terror!"
Camilla puts the handcuffs on Gonzo.

Scooter pulls the lever to lift
him high into the air.
"Drumroll, please!" says Gonzo.

the
GREAT
GONZO

Tapioca Tub of Terror

Gonzo tugs at the handcuffs.

He twists his wrists.

He pulls really hard.

"Just getting them nice and loose!"
he yells to the audience.

Gonzo starts inching closer
to the Tapioca Tub of Terror.
But he is no closer to getting free.
"Maybe if I flap my arms," he says.

Gonzo flaps furiously.
The motion makes the rope
swing back and forth!
Soon, Gonzo completely
loses control!

"HELP!" Gonzo cries as the rope
swings around and around.
The Great Gonzo tries to grab
the curtain to slow down,
but it tears right off.

Gonzo crashes into the set.
The scenery starts to crumble.
Lights, ropes, curtains—
everything tumbles into
the Tapioca Tub of Terror.
Gonzo tumbles in with it all.

The Muppets rush to help.

"Gonzo, are you okay?" they ask.

Gonzo does not answer.

"Speak to us!" cries Kermit.

Gonzo grins widely.

"What a rush!" he says.

"Who knew that magic tricks
make for such great stunts?"